FIFTY-SEVEN BY EIGHT

Samira Gupta

FIFTY-SEVEN BY EIGHT

TRANQUEBAR

TRANQUEBAR PRESS
An imprint of westland ltd
571, Poonamallee High Road, Kamaraj Bhavan, Aminijikarai, Chennai 600 029
1 Floor, Praja Bhavan, 53/2 Bull Temple Road, Basavangudi, Bangalore 560 019
1 Floor, 3-5-1108, Maruthi Complex, Narayanaguda, Hyderabad 500 029
Plot No 102, Marol Coop Ind Estate, Marol, Andheri East, Mumbai 400 059
F-5, Okhla Industrial Area, Phase-1, Mezzanine Floor, New Delhi 110 020

First published by TRANQUEBAR PRESS, 2009

10 9 8 7 6 5 4 3 2 1

ISBN: 978-81-89975-66-1

Printed at : Ajanta Offset & Packagings Ltd., New Delhi

for

Ma, Papa & Parikshit

Acknowledgements

Thanks to all at Westland for believing in my story, especially Nilanjana, Deepthi and Priyanka.
Fifty-Seven by Eight started as a graduation project for Srishti School of Art, Design and Technology. It was here that I discovered my voice, and my book would not have been possible without the support of my faculty members and guides, Radha, Ayisha, Tara, Deb, Avy, Arvind, Rustam, Mr Ravindra, Lloyd and Waseem. I would like to thank my Director, Mrs Geetha Narayanan, for giving me the freedom to literally 'do whatever I wanted'.
Various friends have spared valuable hours of their graduation project/coffee/sleep time to help me figure out my story. Thank you, Viraj, Kinnari, Krittika, Vedika, Amita, Mandira, Rashi and Nanju.
A special thank you to Manisha and Shubho, for guiding and advising me.
Thank you Girish, Rhea, Mr Conz, Mishika and Bali for being around when I needed five hands.
Finally, I would like to thank my family for bearing with my erratic work timings, regular disappearances and late nights.
Thank you Papa for your love and support.
And thank you Ma. You have taught me everything I know. You are the heart of this book.

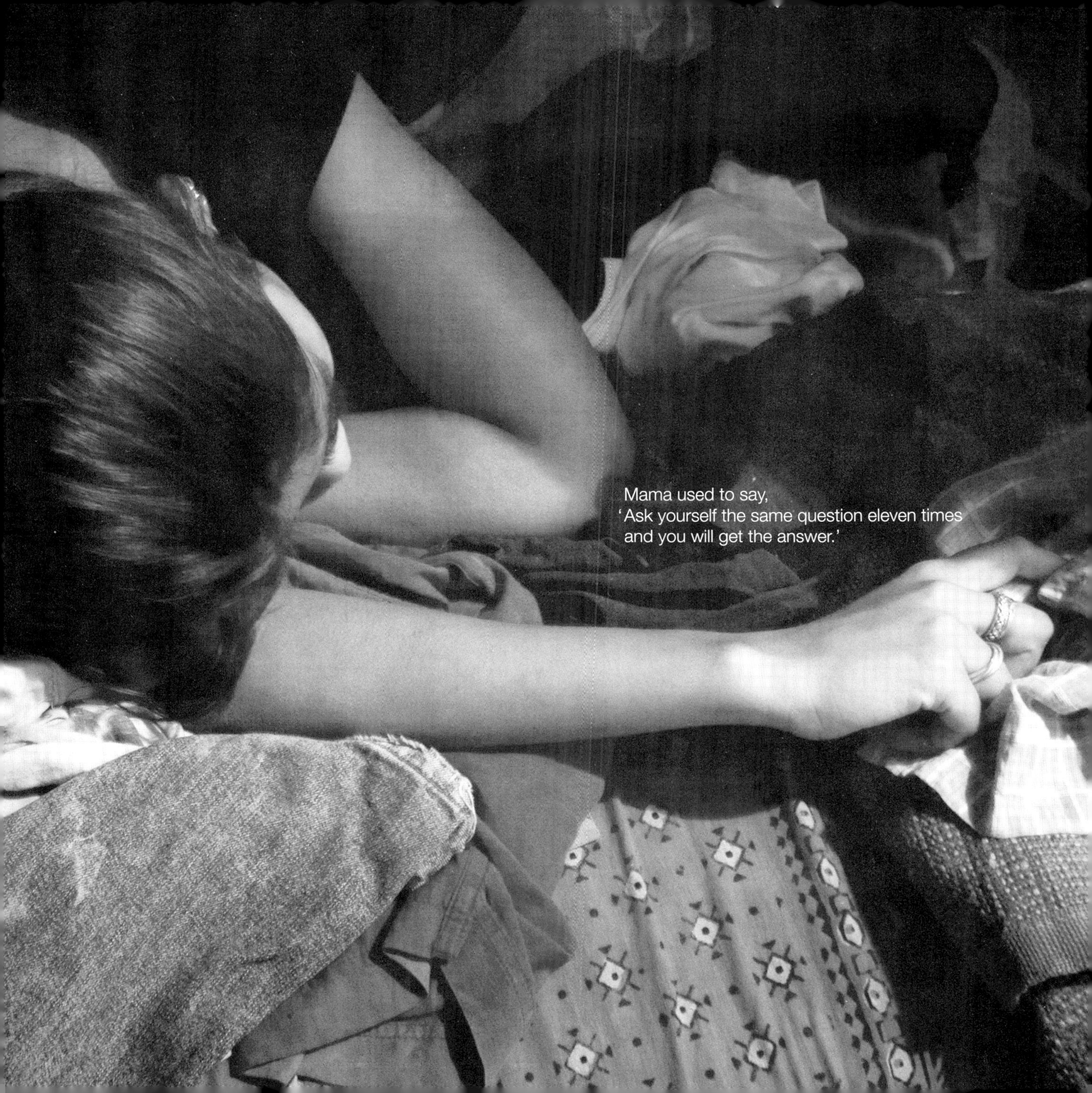

Mama used to say,
'Ask yourself the same question eleven times
and you will get the answer.'

I tried once.

I lived in a big old house on 57/8 Ballygunge Park Lane.

Dadaji owned a big mithai shop.
He was an important man.
Even at home.

OUR SWEETS IN
LONDON

Pranam Dadaji.

Khush raho.

SELLING

Dadi never spoke much in front of Dadaji.

Dadi changed her bangles to match her sari.
Everyday.

History is a constant process of evaluation and revisions. New insights will come in. There's no space for gimmicks
addressing the actor as 'tomader dada'
'My aggression is within limits'
Indian pacer Sree Santh is in Kerala basking in the joy of having his family around him this Onam, but he admits that his heart is in England, where the fight is on for ODI honours against England
On enjoying Onam...
My entire family is down to celebrate Onam, and Raksha Bandhan. My sister is down from Bahrain. This is the first time that we are together after a long time for the festivals. But, I'm not that happy — the ODIs are still happening. I'm training hard for the Twenty20 World Cup that's coming up.

I knew she was coming long before I saw her.
Her keys gave it away.

Everytime.

Mama also had keys.
But they were only for our cupboards.

Dadi hated it when I ran up anc down the stairs.
She said it was not ladylike.

‘Ladki banna seekho’.

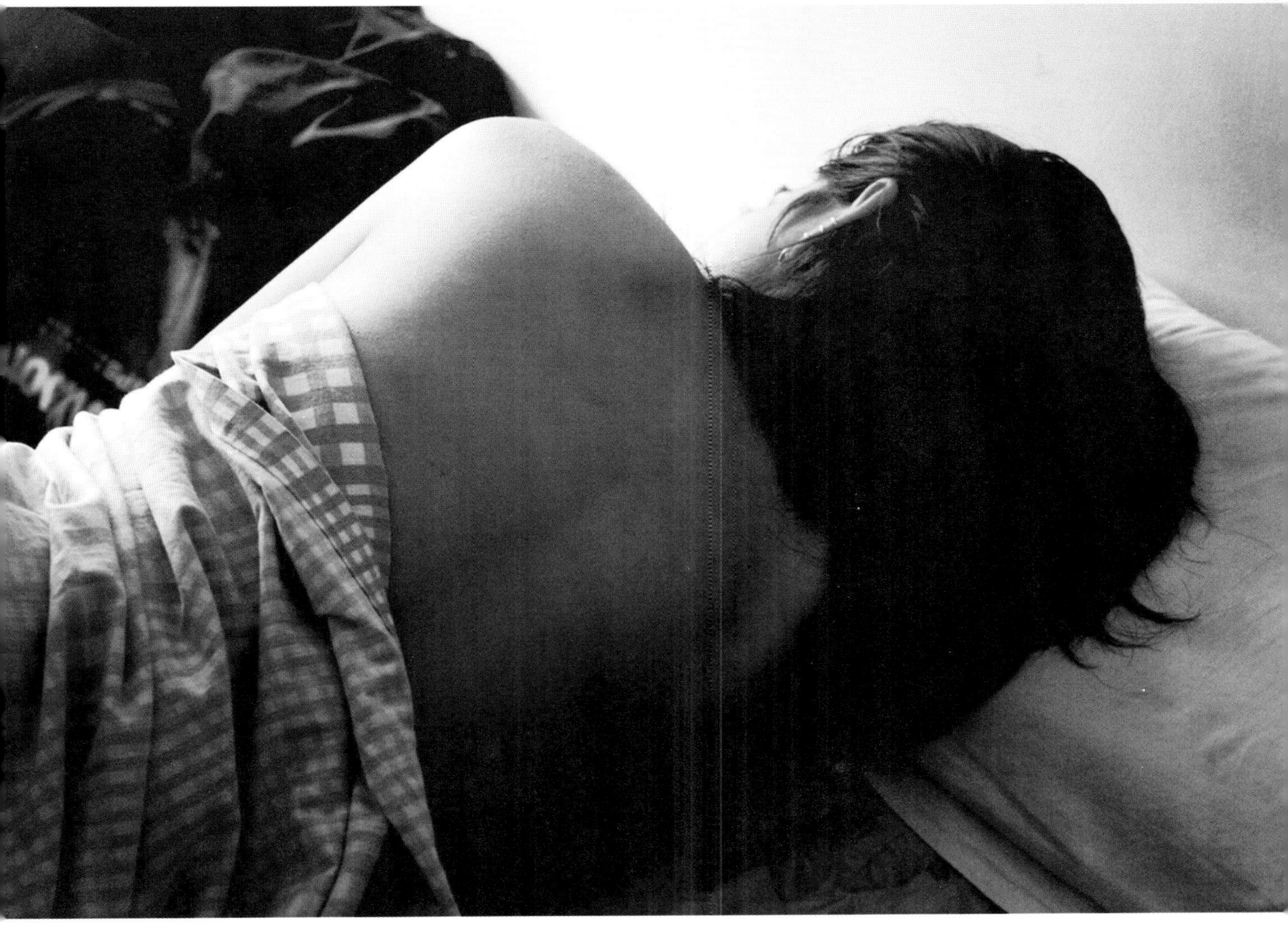

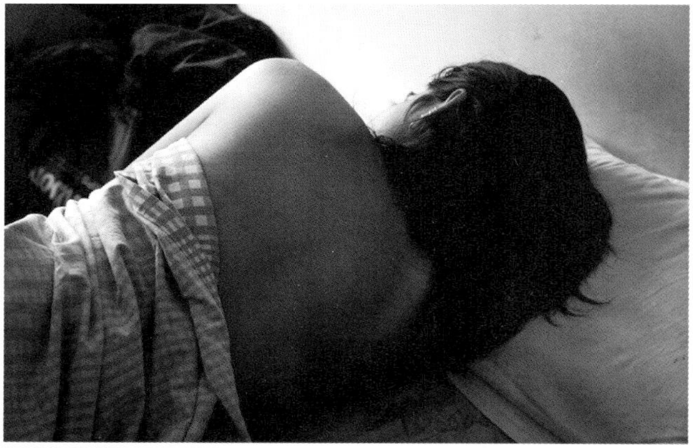
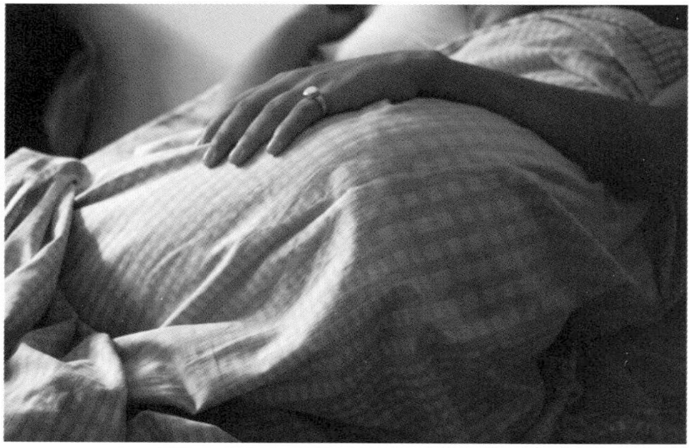
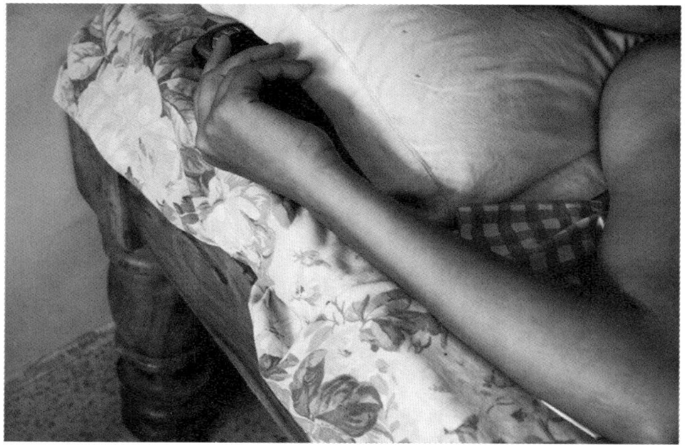
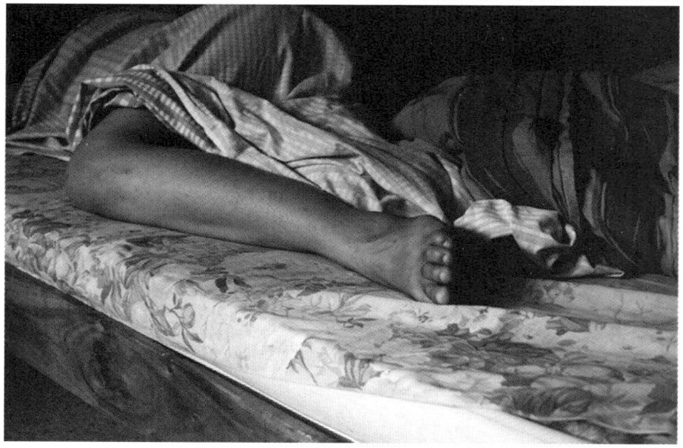

Wonder what she would say now...
And Mama...

The first time I got a ‘Good’ in class.
Mama was very proud of me.

It’s the only thing I’ve preserved from school.
I’ll make her proud again.
Someday.

15.9.95

Mr. Giggle's Shop

I want to buy apresent for mummy,
And I know where to go;
I will go to Mr. Giggle's Shop
And it's right near my home.
Chocolate, Toffees, sweets and Wafers.
Everything he sells,
From thick strong ropes to little dolls,
And from aeroplanes to bells.

Oh! What shall I buy, Oh! What shall I buy,
Oh! what shall I buy for mummy.
Would she like wafers?
Or would she like toffees?
Or will a ribbon do for mummy.
At last I show Mr. Giggles my present,
And he nods and smiles at me.
Two orange wafers and two yellow sweets
And a little brown chocolate forme.

* Good

[illegible] 15/9

Mama was the easiest to find in that house.

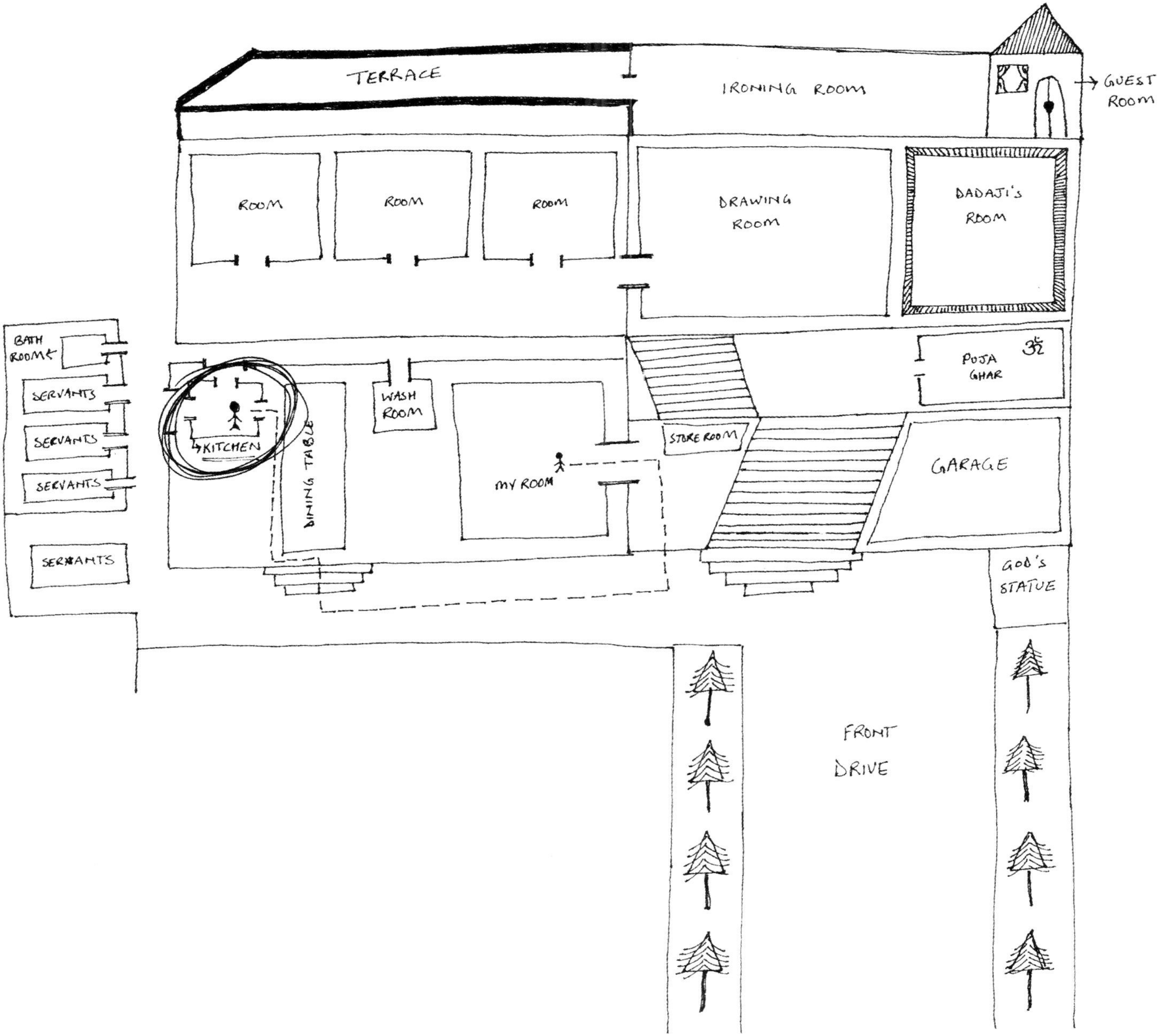
TERRACE
IRONING ROOM
GUEST ROOM
ROOM
ROOM
ROOM
DRAWING ROOM
DADAJI'S ROOM
BATH ROOM
SERVANTS
SERVANTS
SERVANTS
KITCHEN
WASH ROOM
DINING TABLE
MY ROOM
STORE ROOM
POJA GHAR
ॐ
GARAGE
SERVANTS
GOD'S STATUE
FRONT DRIVE

She was always in the kitchen.

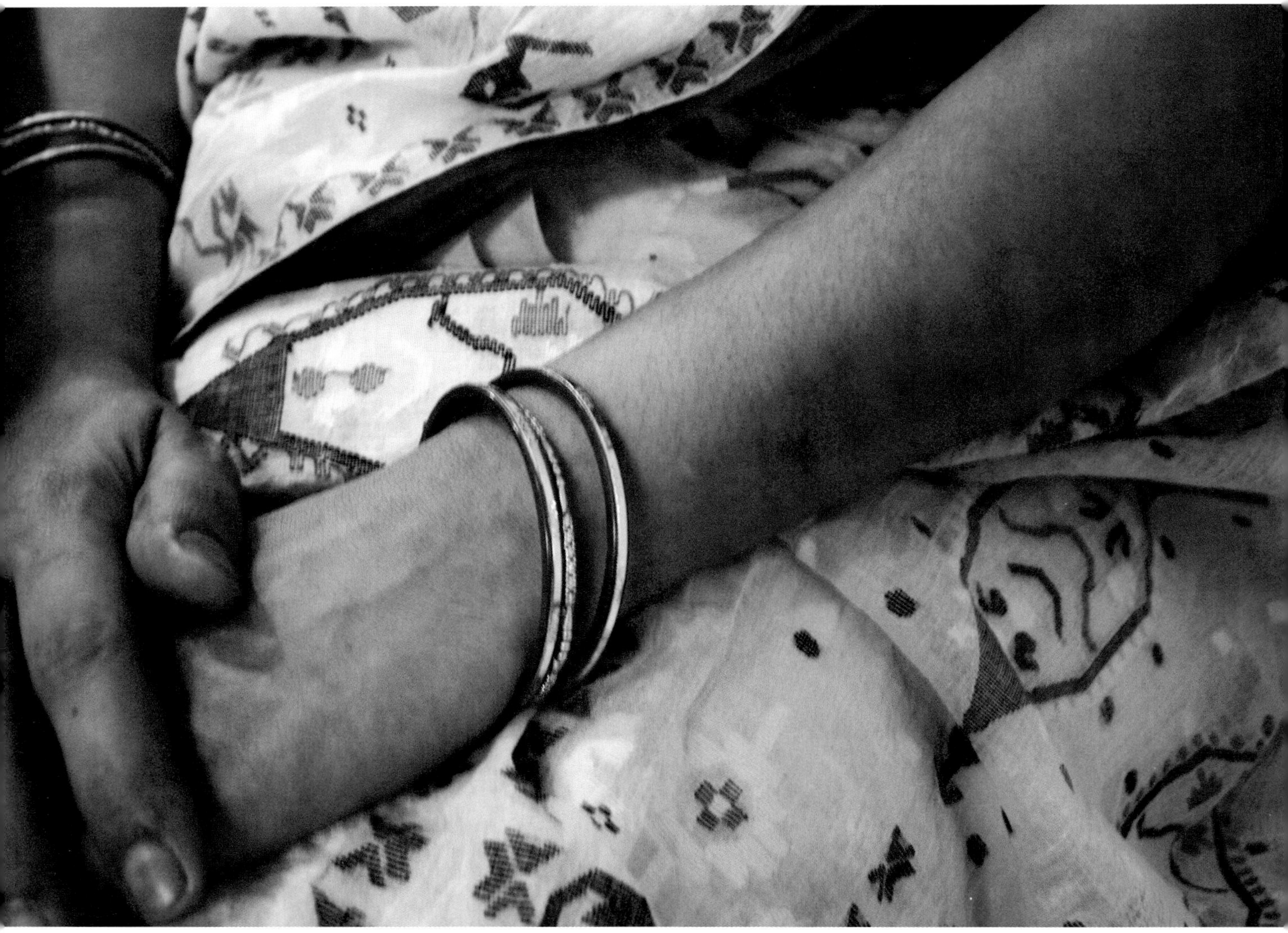

‘We waited till your grandfather came home every night.
Served him. Then ate dinner.’

'Sometimes he would come home really late. I remember many hot summer nights, sitting on those stairs, with no electricity, fanning myself.'

I think Mama made a conscious effort
to keep me away from the kitchen.

I still can't cook.

The light outside casts a soft shadow in my room.
I like to switch off my apartment lights and sit in semi darkness.
Then my world seems mellow. Soft and new again.
Everything looks different and yet the same.
Every night I trace new shadows on the floor.
Every night I spend time with myself.

Trainspotting
Choose your future.
The Who
STONES
WITHSTAND
DIVORCE
SLANDER
RIP-OFFS
SLAGGING
UNDER-AGE SEX
ALCOHOL
DRUGS

STONES

Where did I go wrong?

This used to be my cupboard.
I had pretty flowers on it.
ALL my clothes fit in here.
I also had a key to it.

I never called my friends home.
Dadaji always got angry.
I think we made too much noise.

That's why birthdays were so special.

[illegible]

I tasted freedom in little things.

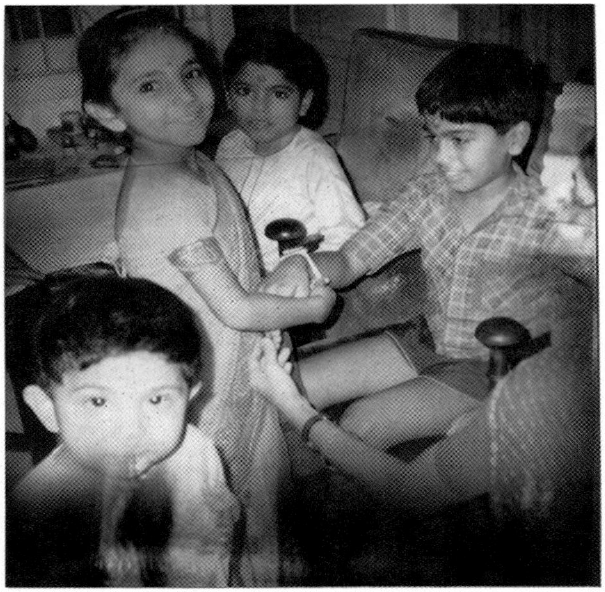

gifts during rakhi

trip to the zoo

Sunday morning drives to
the Race Course

hanging on the balcony railing

The front drive was my battleground.

Race you to the main door!

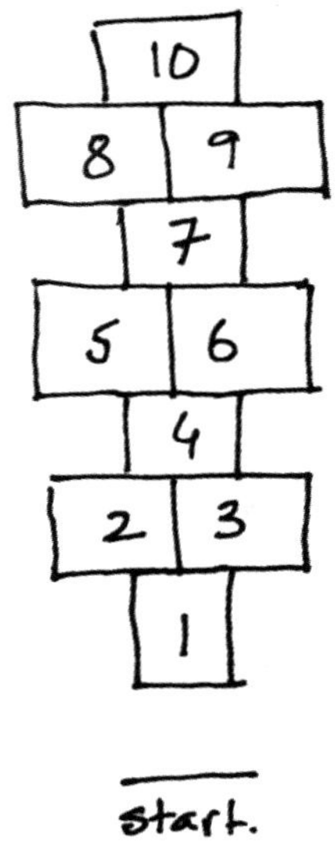
10
8
9
7
5
6
4
2
3
1
start.

MY battleground.

12. 2. 93

Homework

Question

What do you do everyevening at home?

Answer

Every evening after school I eat lunch. After that my mother asks me to sleep for sometime. If I dont feel sleepy then she allows me to play. All my brothers sleep in the afternoon so I play on my own.

Then in the evening we all skate on the front drive. It is a lot of fun. We always have competitions and marathons but I never win. The straps are hard so sometimes we get cuts. But nobody ever complains. Skating is fun. I skate every evening at home.

I play with my brothers every evening.

The deepest cuts were envied.
Somehow my cuts never caught their attention.

295

295

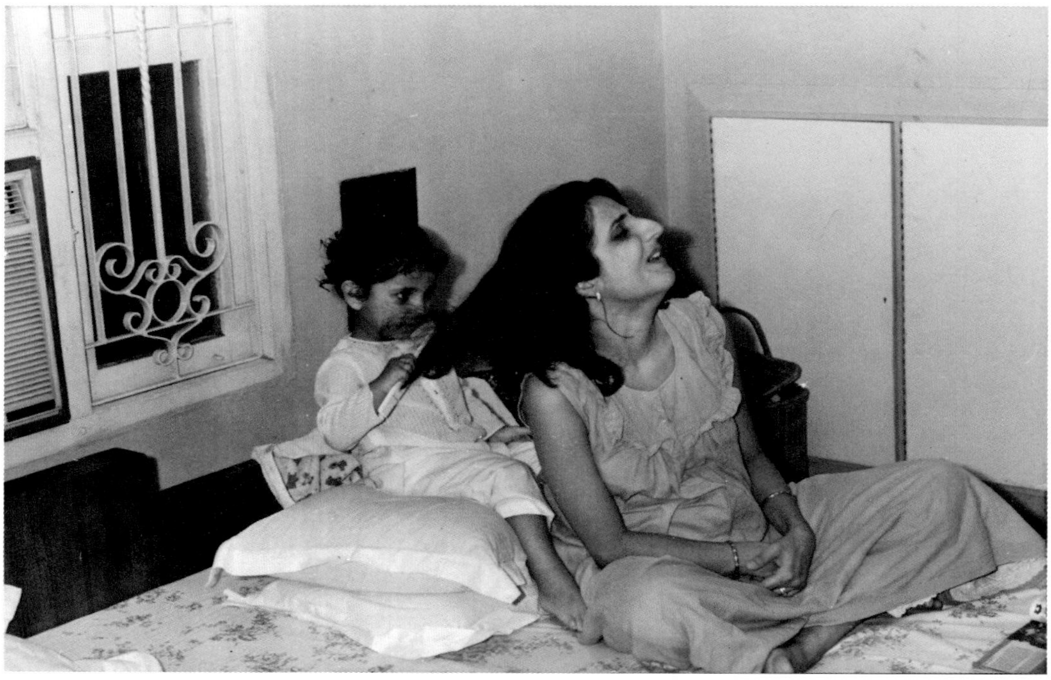

Once Mama and I got our periods together.
She was not allowed into the kitchen or the puja ghar.
I couldn't go out to play.

We spent a lot of time together.
It was nice to see Mama so relaxed and happy.

The House of God.

Our puja ghar was between the ground floor and the first floor.

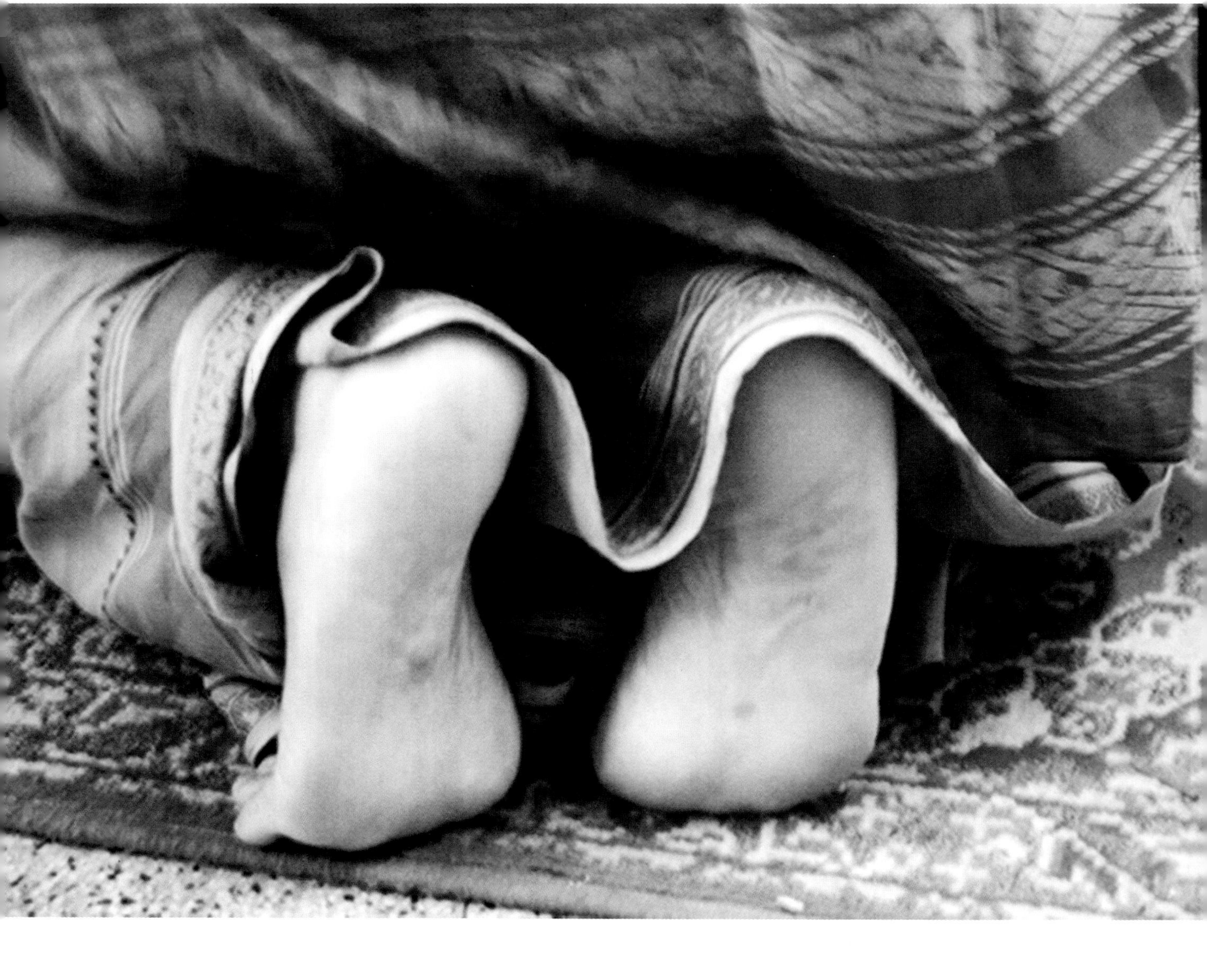

Mama used to say, ‘That’s because God does not take sides.’

I believed her.
God never helped Papa.

I don't believe in God.

When everyone slept in the afternoon,
I spied on my neighbours.

Mr Das and Archana di

Aparna Dutta

Rahul Ramaswamy
Panty
Me

Old Mr Das and Archana di.

I would spy on them for hours, but I never saw them

My brother claimed he saw Mr Das once. I think he lied.

Rumour has it that they still live there.

Rahul wore his shorts really really high.
We used to tease him, saying he didn't need a shirt.
My brothers made him cry once.

Pronounced: 'Oporna Dotho'.
She spent a summer with her grandparents here.
I used to bully her a lot.
I think I made her cry once.

My terrace overlooked the Ballygunge Army Camp.
I could look into one of the guard's quarters.

And there resided Panty. Aptly nicknamed.
He slept outside his house on a khatiya in his kachchas.

I would wait for him to fall asleep and then shout

PAAAAANTIEE

and duck.

He never got used to it. I never got tired of it.

MACHINE GHAR

Ramu used to live here.

It smelt of petrol, Ramu's sweat and old clothes.
Perfect place to hide from the elders.
They never came to the servants' quarters.

I was small enough to not be noticed, so I listened to all their gossip.
That was my job and my brothers relied on me to do it well.

Dadaji never found out.
He didn't like us mixing too much with the servants.
Especially the girls.

So my job was 'top secret'.
And I never failed my brothers.

Sometimes I still like to spy.

STONES

men make me feel beautiful. Men make me feel ugly. Sometimes I feel so damn special. Sometimes I don't feel so damn special. Most of the times I feel like an afterthought. Men make me feel beautiful. Men make me feel ugly. Men make me feel like an afterthought. When I wash my hair I look very nice. I think I looked beautiful. I desperately wanted to look pretty. But then they laugh and all that. I feel really stupid. I hate feeling stupid. I try not let it bother me. I try not to let their opinion bother me. It bothers me that it bothers me. Then sometimes they say nice things. The way he touches my cheek. The way he smiles at me. There is no consistency. Men make me feel beautiful. Men make me feel ugly. Maybe thats the law of nature. You must feel bad to feel good. You must feel good to feel bad. I feel bad so many times. Wonder when I will begin to feel good. I wish I had nicer hair. It's so difficult. Men make me feel beautiful. Men make me feel ugly. Men make me feel like an afterthought. I was never like this before. These things never really bothered me. Why did it have to change. Now I can't make my own decisions. I have to ask. I need to ask. Men make me feel beautiful and ugly.

men make me fe
me feel ugly. So
special. Sometimes
special. Most of th
afterthought. Men
Men make me fe
feel like an aft
my hair I look ver
beautiful. I desperat
But then they laug
really stupid. I hate
let it bother me. I
bother me. It both
me. Then sometimes
way he touches my
at me. There is no c
feel beautiful. Men m
thats the law of
to feel good. You m
I feel bad so man
begin to feel good
It's so difficult. Men
Men make me fee
feel like an af
this before. These
me. Why did it ha
make my own decisi
to ask. Men make m

eautiful. Men make
mes I feel so damn
don't feel so damn
nes I feel like an
me feel beautiful.
gly. Men make me
ght. When I wash
ce. I think I looked
vanted to look pretty.
d all that. I feel
ling stupid. I try not
ot to let their opinion
e that it bothers
say nice things. The
k. The way he smiles
ncy. Men make me
me feel ugly. Maybe
. You must feel bad
feel good to feel bad.
es. Wander when I will
ish I had nicer hair.
ke me feel beautiful.
ly. Men make me
ght. I was never like
never really bothered
change. Now I can't
I have to ask. I need
beautiful and ugly.

Men make me feel beautiful. Men make me feel ugly. Sometimes I feel so damn special. Sometimes I don't feel so damn special. Most of the times I feel like an afterthought. Men make me feel beautiful. Men make me feel ugly. Men make me feel like an afterthought. When I wash my hair I look very nice. I think I looked beautiful. I desperately wanted to look pretty. But then they laugh and all that. I feel really stupid. I hate feeling stupid. I try not let it bother me. I try not to let their opinion bother me. It bothers me that it bothers me. Then sometimes they say nice things. The way he touches my cheek. The way he smiles at me. There is no consistency. Men make me feel beautiful. Men make me feel ugly. Maybe thats the law of nature. You must feel bad to feel good. You must feel good to feel bad. I feel bad so many times. Wander when I will begin to feel good. I wish I had nicer hair. It's so difficult. Men make me feel beautiful. Men make me feel ugly. Men make me feel like an afterthought. I was never like this before. These things never really bothered me. Why did it have to change. Now I can't make my own decisions. I have to ask. I need to ask. Men make me feel beautiful and ugly.

BEAUTY
Rs. 170/-

A boy in a fete once gave me a paper heart.
It was soft to touch.

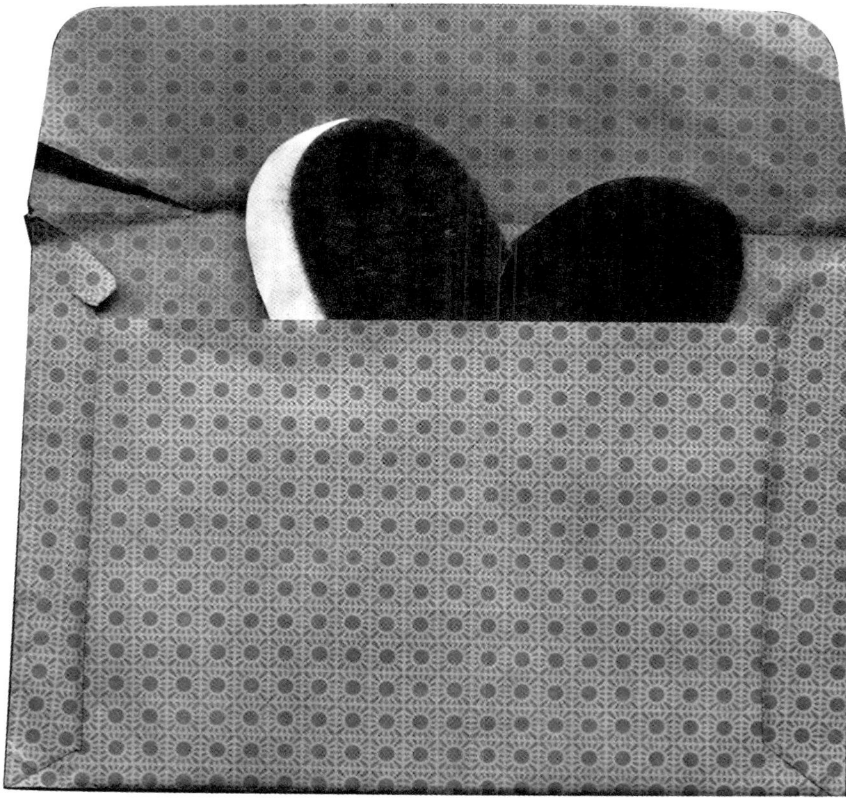

I felt beautiful.

Then I wanted to look beautiful.

Parlour : 475-7025
Resi. : 247-3898

7522

JUNE TOMKYNS

Beauty Parlour

26/2, BALLYGUNGE ~~CIRCULAR ROAD~~
1st Floor, Suit No. 3
CALCUTTA-700 019

Name ____________________

Quantity	DESCRIPTION	Rs.	P.
	Shampoo	75	00
	Blow dry	95	00
	TOTAL	170	00

Date 3/2/99 .... Signature

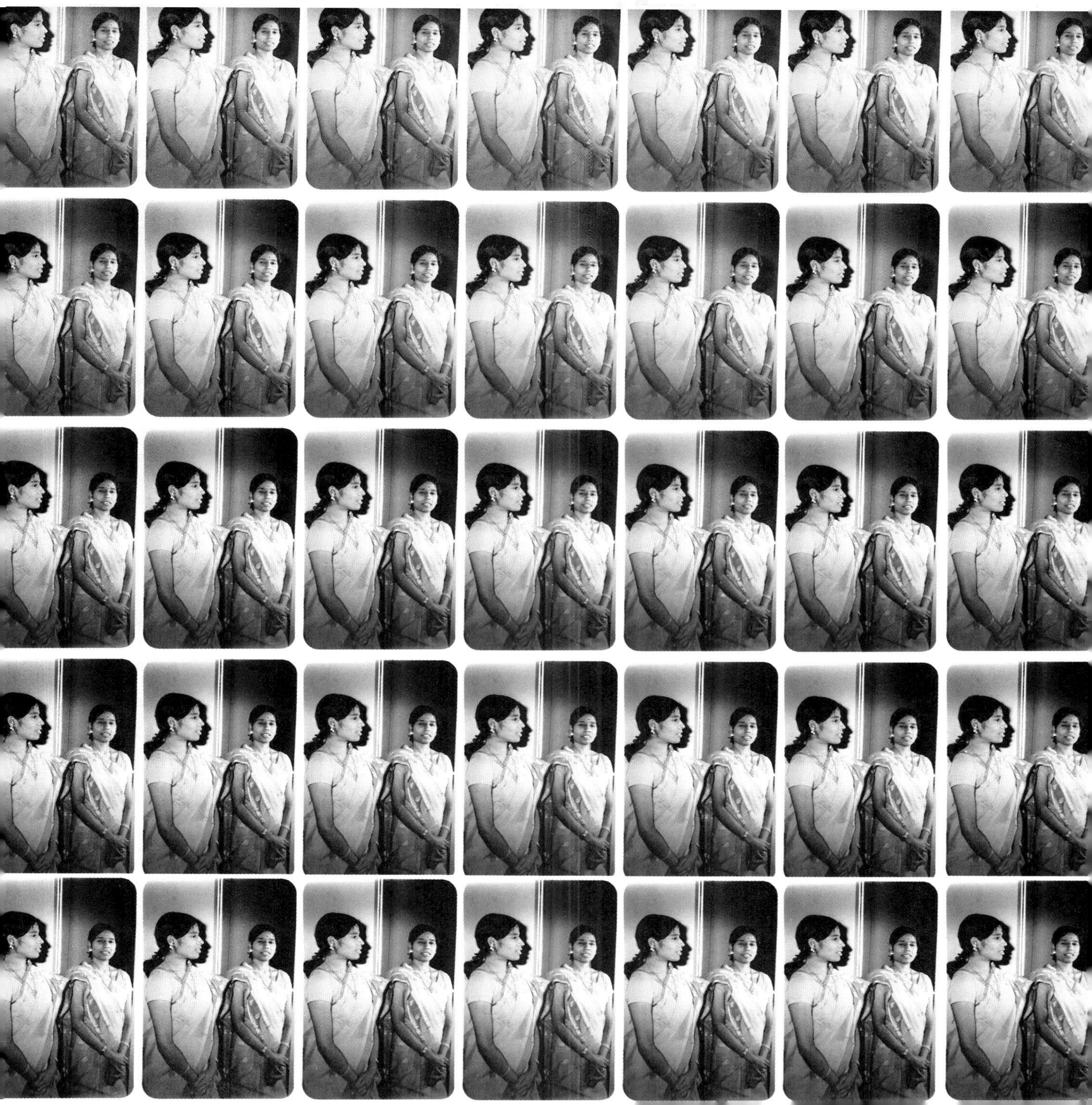

Every Wednesday
7pm onwards
5697
Ladies Night
Complementry Drink
Every Wednesday
7pm onwards
5697
Ladies Night
Complementry Drink
Every Wednesday
7pm onwards
5697
Ladies Night
Complementry Drink
Every Wednesday
7pm onwards
5697
Ladies Night
Complementry Drink
Every Wednesday
7pm onwards
5697
Ladies Night
Complementry Drink
Every Wednesday
7pm onwards
5697
Ladies Night
Complementry Drink
Every Wednesday
7pm onwards
5697
Ladies Night
Complementry Drink
Every Wednesday
7pm onwards
5697
Ladies Night
Complementry Drink
Every Wednesday
7pm onwards
5697
Ladies Night
Complementry Drink

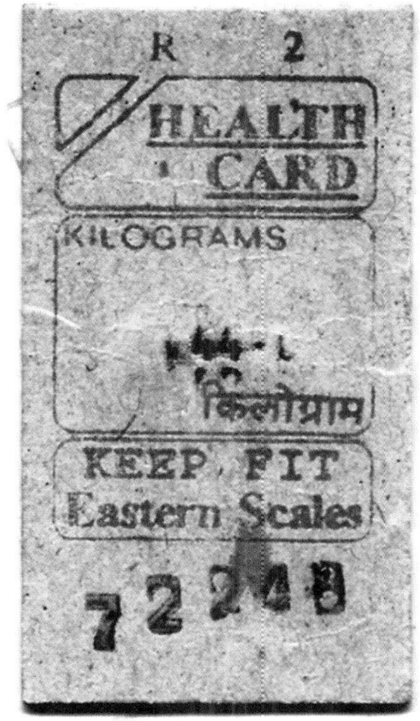

Forty-four kilograms.

JANUARY 2001

1 *Monday*

Why can't mama understand
Sometimes that I have
a life of my <u>OWN</u>!

2 *Tuesday*

JAN 2001

S	M	T	W	T	F	S
	1	2	3	4	5	6
7	8	9	10	11	12	13
14	15	16	17	18	19	20
21	22	23	24	25	26	27
28	29	30	31			

ugly. Sometimes I ... beautiful.
Sometimes I don't feel so ... Men make
Most of the times I feel so damn
thought. Men make me feel so damn
make me feel like an
feel like a ... ugly. Men make me feel beautiful.
my hair ... When I wash
beautiful. ... I think I looked
But then
really stupid.
let it bother
bother
me. Then
way
at me.
That's to feel
to feel
I feel
begin to
It's so
Men make
feel light.
this never
me.
make
to ... beautiful

Papa used to comb my hair for hours to make it shine.
Then he would tie it up in a tight ponytail.
I thought I looked very nice like that.

Papa said I looked like a princess.

BJ6402

Beautiful.

Sometimes
when it's really quiet,
I listen.

There is something about the wind
just before it's going to rain.

It's calming.

Mama lied for me once.

No. 18139
METRO CINEMA
CIRCLE
ADMN. 20.00
A. TAX. 14.00
S. CH 1.00
Tax Prepaid in liau of W. B. E. Stamps
35.00
Date
SATURDAY NOON
This hall to be retained till end of performance. Tickets sold for date and time of parformance only. Money cancel be refunded.
Patrons whose ticket once Punched will not be allowed to leave primises even during Interval

I wanted to go for a film with cnly my friends
and Dadaji would never have agreed.

So Mama didn't tell him.

I thought Mama was very strong and brave.

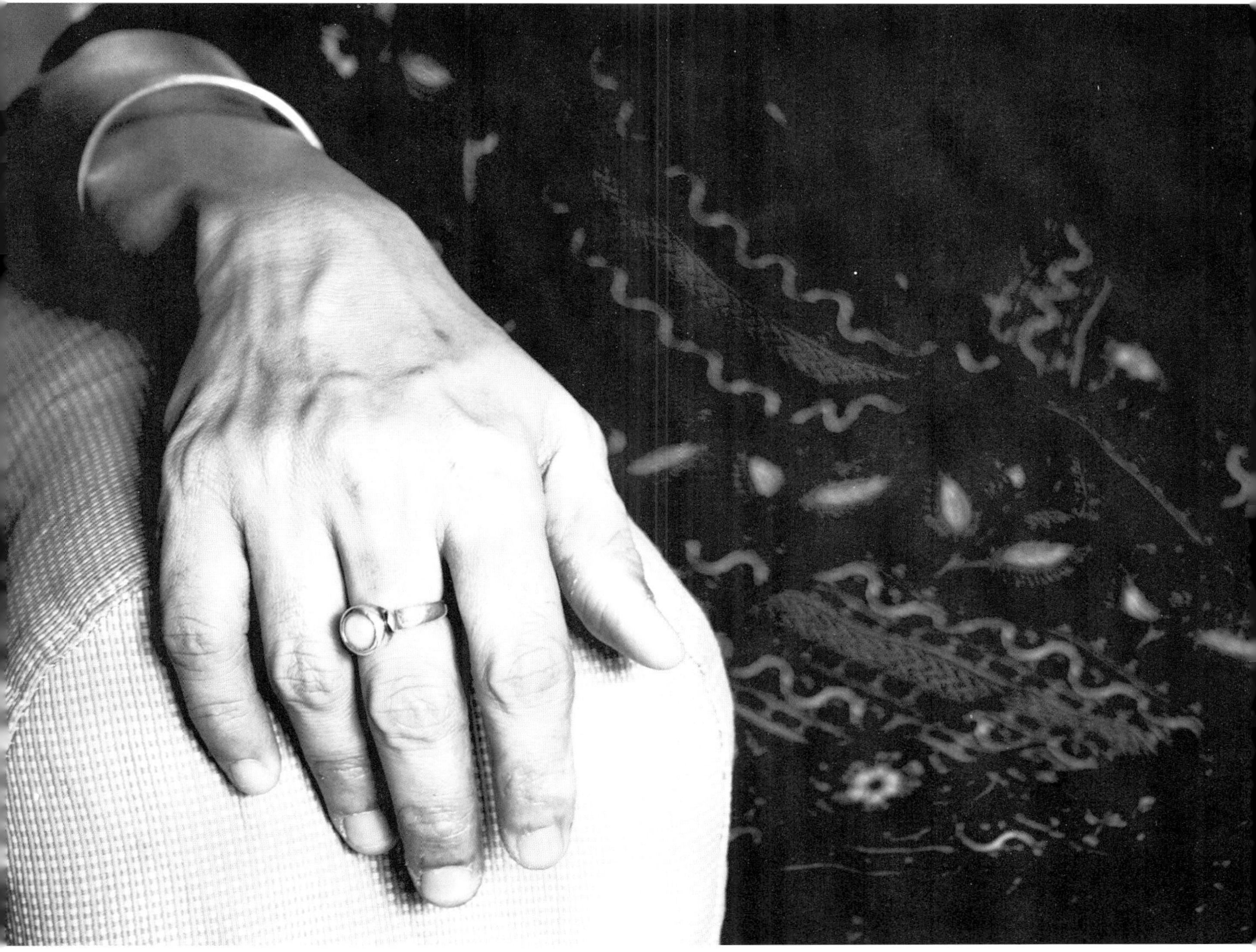

MEET JOE
BLACK

I felt grown up sitting in that dark theatre
watching Brad Pitt.

That day, I didn't want to go back home.

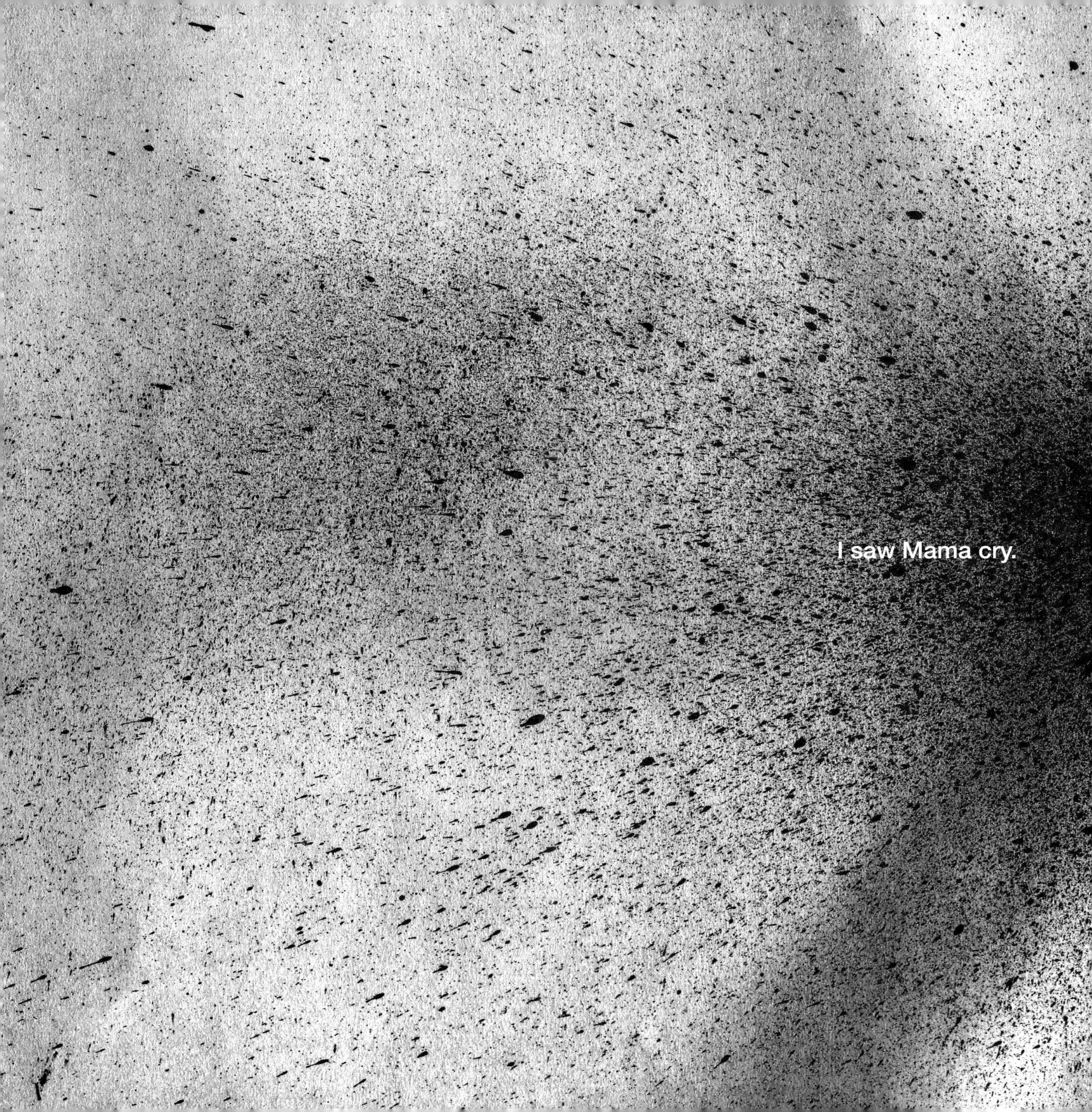

I saw Mama cry.

நீதியின் மீதும் சத்தியத்தின் மீதும் அலாதிப்
பற்றுள்ள நீங்கள் ஒடுக்கபபடுகிற,
கொடுமைக்கு ஆளாகிற எளியோரின்பால்
பரிவு கொண்டவர்.

Love of justice and truth; you will defend the weak against oppression and tyranny.

I tasted freedom in big things.

The first time I won a race.

295

Receipt No. D **11707**

PHONE : { 247-5668 / 247-5326

MODERN HIGH SCHOOL FOR GIRLS

78, SYED AMIR ALI AVENUE, CALCUTTA-700 019.

Received with thanks from Mr./Mrs. Samira Gupta - VIII - B

a sum of Rs. 350/- (Rupees Three hundred fifty only)

only, by Cash/~~Cheque~~ in payment of the School fees of his/her ward/s as per bill

No. 6287 attached herewith.

MODERN H.SCHOOL FOR GIRLS, CAL. ★ RECEIVED Date........19

Dated 14 - 1 - 1998.

The first time I paid my school fees myself.

No. 18137
METRO CINEMA
CIRCLE
ADMN. 20.00
A. TAX 14.00
S. CH 1.00
35.00
Tax Prepaid in liau of W. B. E. Stamps
Date
SATURDAY NOON
This hall to be retained till end of performance. Tickets sold for date and time of performance only. Money cancel be refunded.
Patrons whose ticket once Punched will not be allowed to leave primises even during Interval
No. 18139
No. 18140

The first time I went for a movie alone.

And then the second.

Enjoy Coca-Cola Coke TRADEMARKS REGD

1115 Rs. 35.00

The Lighthouse

FRONT CIRCLE

Adm.	Rs. 20.00
A. Tax	Rs. 14.00
S. Charge	Re. 1.00
Total	Rs. 35.00

PER TAX LIEU OF MPS PAID

This half to be retained till end of performance. Management reserves the right to refuse admission. Money can not be refunded.

SUNDAY NIGHT

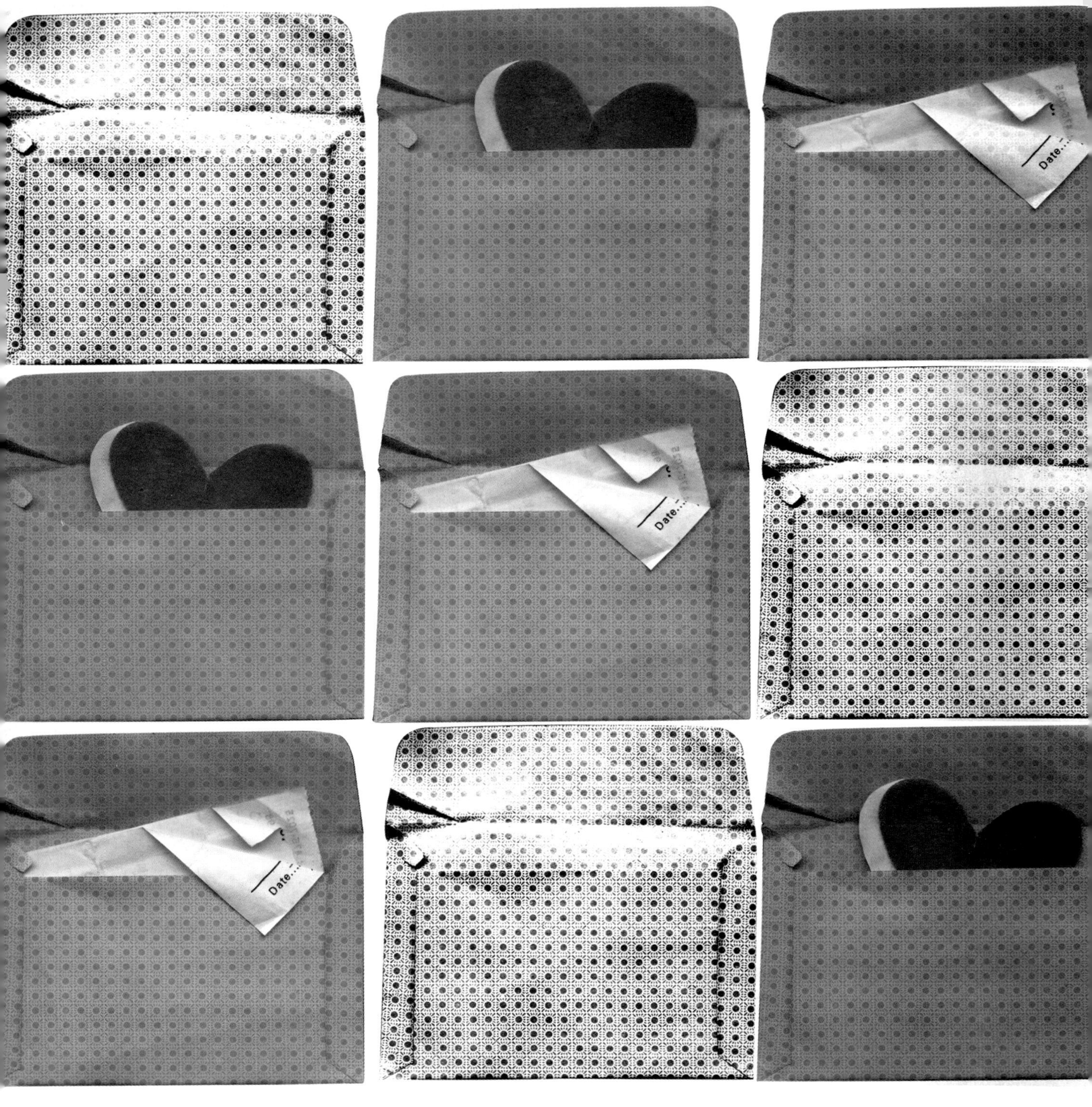
Date...
Date...
Date...
Date...

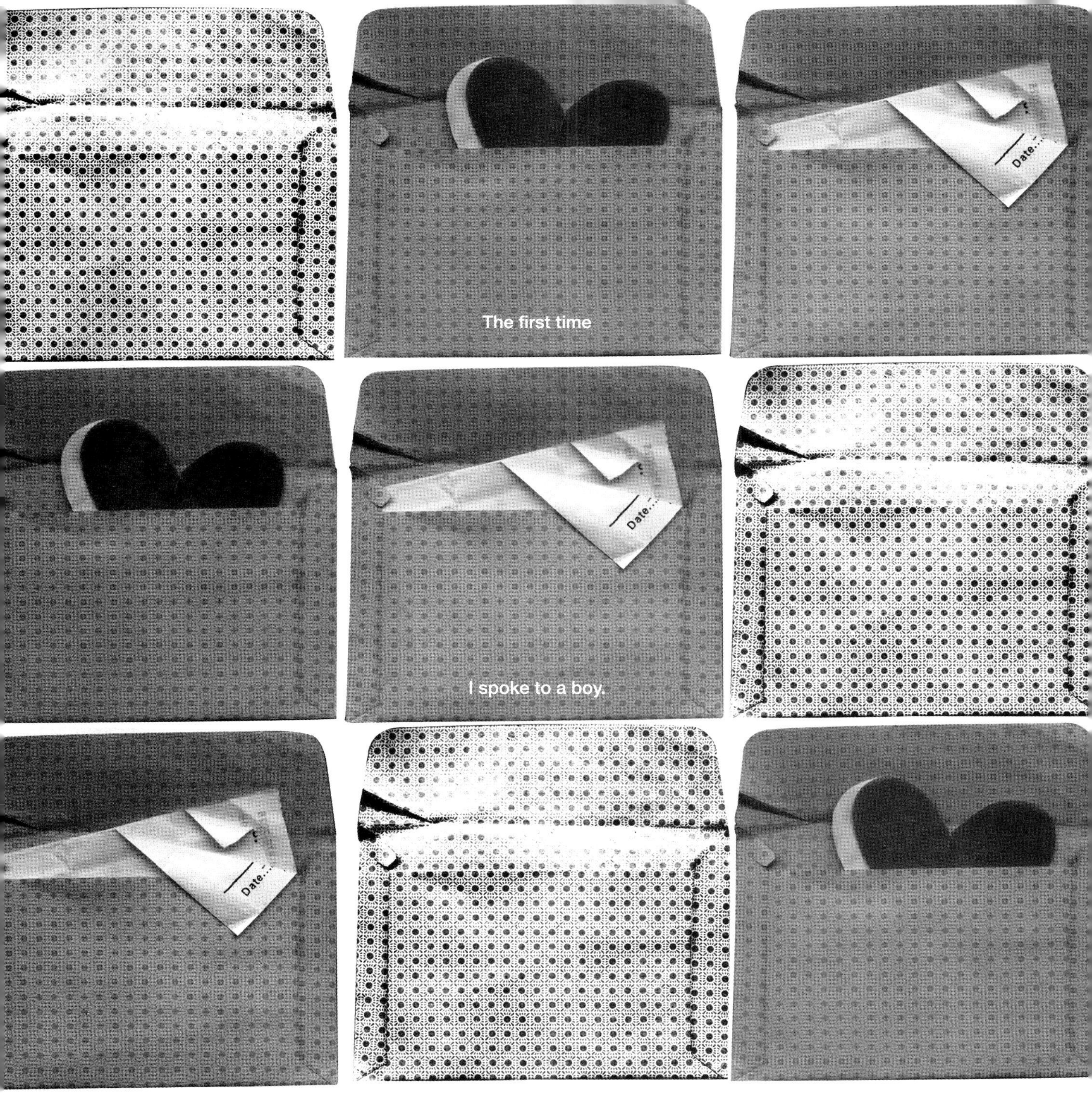
The first time
I spoke to a boy.

The first time I left home to be on my own.

To be alone.

It's good to cry.

There has to be a reason behind everything.

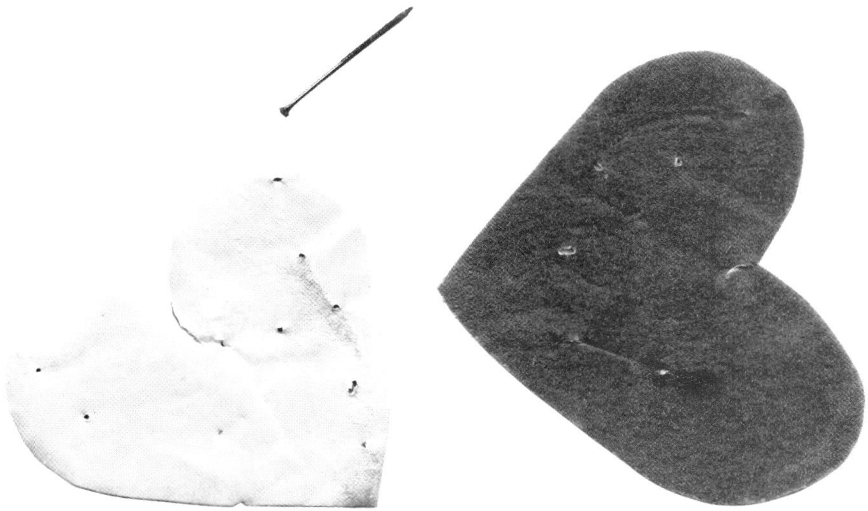

He kept calling me a NAG, you are a ~~ng~~ nag. Stop asking me
so many questions. Why do you call me when I'm in a meeting.
I was worried. I didn't know. You're such a nag. I'm sorry.
Stop pointing out all my faults. I was just asking. I'm sorry. NO,
I can't meet you today. NO. I told you I can't. So what can
I do? Why do you want to know? Stop interfering. I can't help
it. I don't need to answer. I'm sorry. I didn't mean to upset
you. Atleast listen to me. Can't you just shut up sometimes?
What do you want to know? I don't know. NAG. Stop it.
Just STOP IT. STOP nagging me all the time. WHY CAN'T
YOU JUST shut up. I don't know why we are together. I
don't care anymore. It's ALL your fault. Whatever. I don't
want to be with you. I DON'T CARE. You are ~~a~~ nag. Change
yourself. MAYBE I AM A NAG. he just kept calling me a nag.
NAG. NAG. NAG. NAG. NAG. I need to change myself. Maybe
I shouldn't call so often. It's all my fault. It's all YOUR
fault. I should give him more space. I NEED MY SPACE.
Don't call me when I'm working. It disturbs me. No
ONE in office knows I'm seeing you. I don't want to tell
anyone. It might affect his work. It's all my fault. I
am a NAG. I need to change. I'm going to change.
Why can't he like me the way I am. Why can't
YOU like me the way I am. I don't know. My
head hurts. Maybe I'll sleep for a while. Maybe he will
call me back. And then everything will be okay.
I can't even tell anyone. Who should I talk to? No
NO he'll get angry. I think I'll just sleep for sometime now
Maybe I'm a NAG.

I AM
AVAILABLE

I'm allowed to have one weakness.

As long as no one knows.

GOOD HABITS अच्छी आदतें

EARLY TO RISE
सवेरे उठना | सकाळी उठणे

CLEANLINESS
दाँत साफ करना | दात घासणे

EXERCISE
व्यायाम करना | व्यायाम करणे

DAILY BATH
स्नान करना | अंघोळ करणे

PRAYER
प्रार्थना करना | प्रार्थना करणे

BREAKFAST
नाष्टा करना | न्याहारी करणे

STUDYING
पढाई करना | अभ्यास करणे

PLAYING
खेलना | खेळणे

HELPS OTHERS
दुसरोंकी सहायता करना | दुसऱ्याला मदत करणे

TAKES PART IN SOCIAL ACTIVITIES
समाज कार्य मे भाग लेना | समाजकार्य करणे

REGULAR READING
रोज पढना | नियमित अभ्यास

EARLY TO BED
समय पर सोना | वेळेवर झोपणे

Men make me feel

feel like an

feel like an

AFTERTHOUGHT

AFTER THOUGHT

THOUGHT AFTER

AFTER THOUGHT

THOUGHT AFTER

I should never have eft home.

there are so many cobwebs on the ceiling... and in the
corners... where do these spiders come from? maybe
it's the dirt. My room is filthy. Can't remember the
last time I cleaned it. I hope I'm not talking aloud.
That would be funny. That old house had so many
damn cobwebs. I remember ramu once telling me
that cobwebs healed wounds. I was tempted to try
once. But it looked so dirty. He must have been
pulling a fast one. Bastard! I have to clean these
cobwebs. Maybe tomorrow. When I can think straight.
My head is spinning really badly. लड़की बनना सीखो।
भगवान से डरो। Oh god.... forgive me for I have sinned.
So how the hell does god know what I'm doing
anyway... Who cares! As long as mama doesn't get to
know. Then I'm screwed! Imagine her walking in now..
I won't be able to concentrate on what she's saying.
I'm already seeing in multiples of 3. Imagine three
mamas lecturing me together. I think that's where the
idea of surround sound came from. The guy who
invented it must have been stoned. Shit those
cobwebs are flying. I have to clean them. But my
broom isn't long enough. What the hell! Know
what I feel like eating? LADOO! I hate these
cravings.. I hate missing home. I think I only
miss mama a lot. Man I need to grow up....
and clean those cobwebs... before this place
looks like a hollywood set for a bad horror flick...

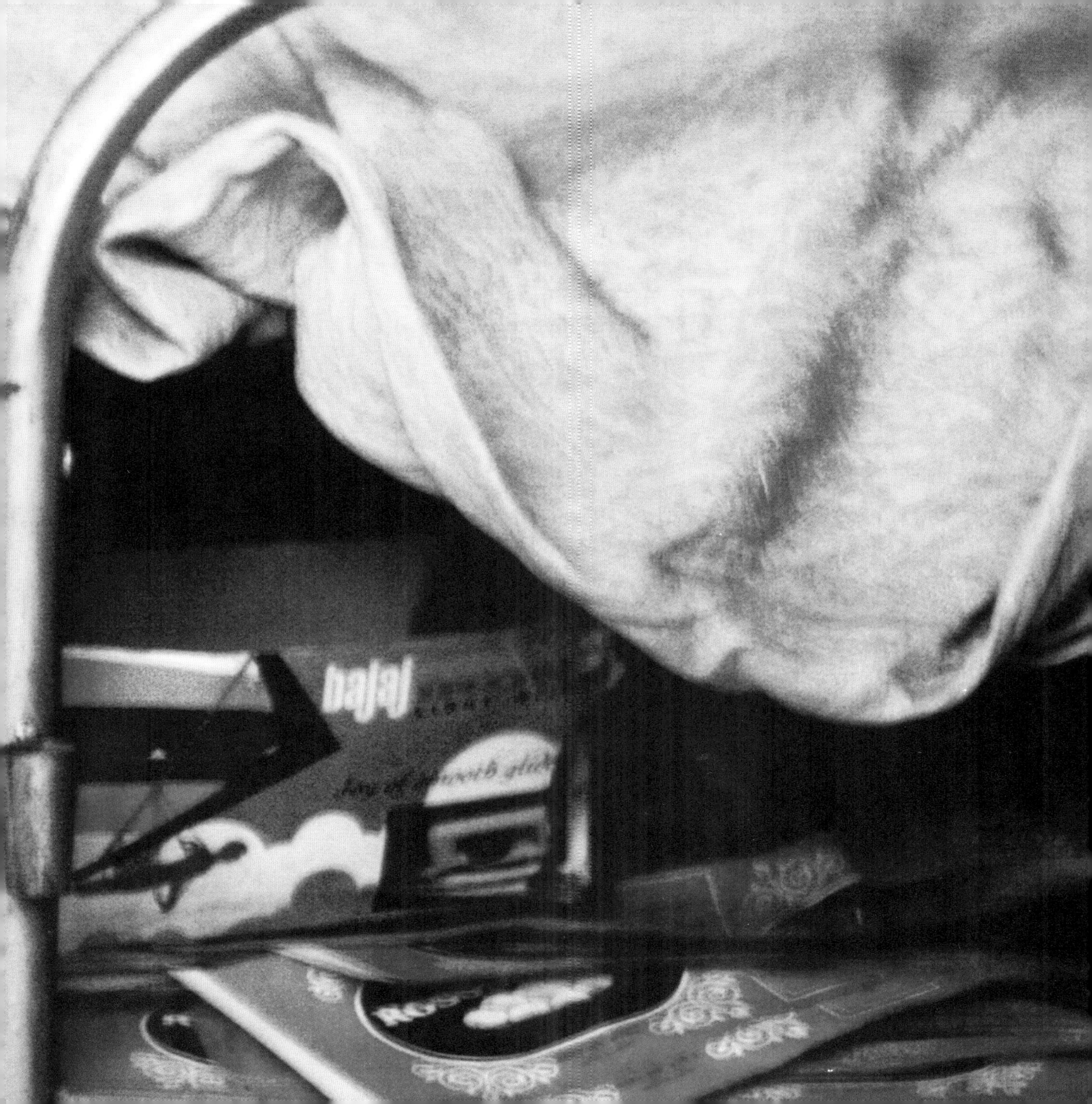

Wednesday 3

Thursday 4

T	F	S
1	2	3
8	9	10
15	16	17
22	23	24

FEB 2001

Hey! Considering everything that's happened this [illegible] time. Still [illegible] last day in Cal - last day of vacation [illegible] hit the [illegible] called a [illegible] went to Ballygunge - had lunch - came home - relaxed - went online - was having fun [illegible] Computer [illegible] - closed - [illegible] crashed [illegible] Really don't wanna [illegible] so stupid - [illegible] [illegible] that it's [illegible] [illegible] [illegible] went to [illegible] tomorrow [illegible] SUNDAY! [illegible]

While you sleep
I think
I forget
I leave behind my mistakes
I leave behind my broken past
I leave behind everything
I close my eyes
To feel

I close my eyes
To heal

choose your future.
The Who
STONES
WITHSTAND
DIVORCE+SLANDER
RIP-OFF+SLAGGING
UNDER-AGE SEX
ALCOHOL+DRUGS

There is a sense of freedom in living alone.
Sometimes I sleep late.
Sometimes I wake up late.
Sometimes I sleep a lot.
And then sometimes,
I just can't sleep.

I think I'll go back home.

HOME.

Dadaji's big mithai shop does not look so big anymore.

Nor does my old house.

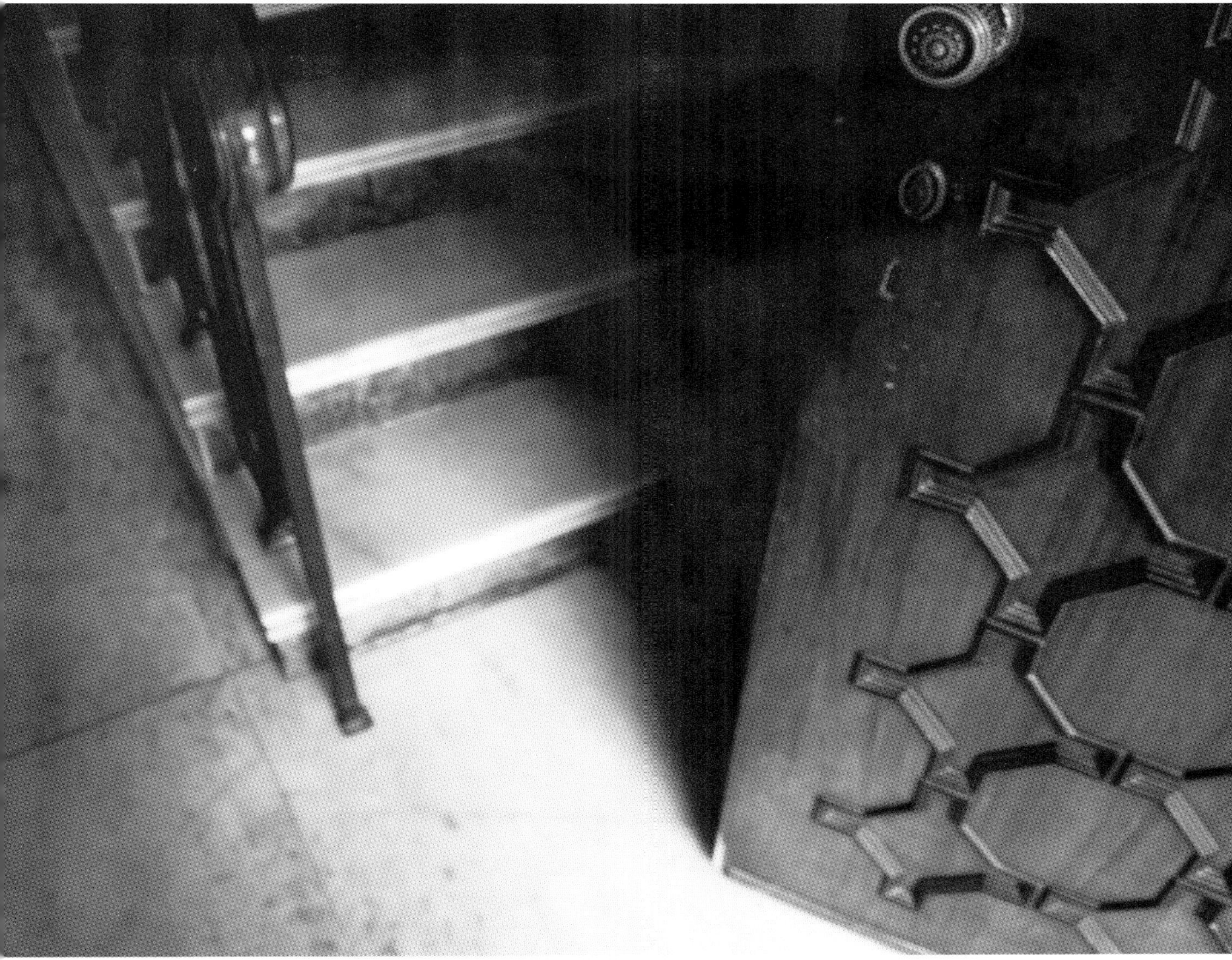

Dadi?

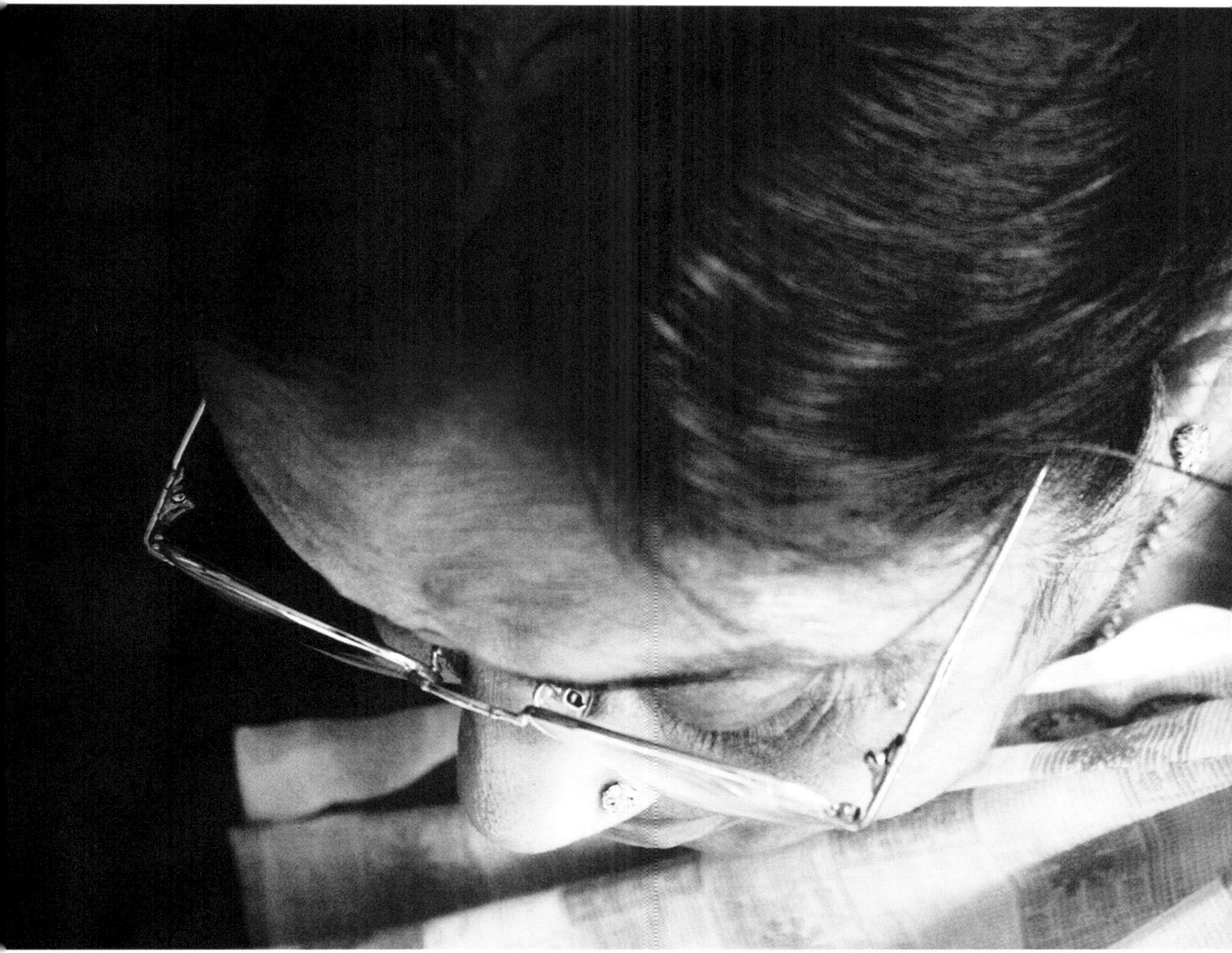

Pranam.

‘Kaisi ho beta?’

‘Where is everyone?’

‘Sab chale gaye, tumhari terah.’

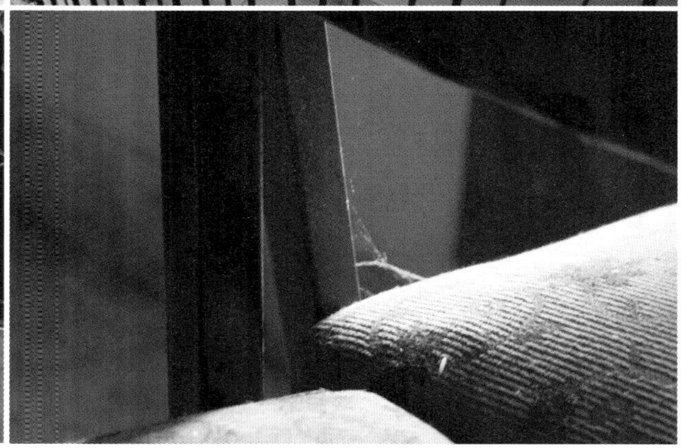

'Sab bandh hai. Chaabi mere paas hai.'

My old room...

The switchboard has still not been repaired.

Remnants of the past linger in the present.
When nothing has changed and yet nothing is the same.

I can't stay here. I have to leave.

SMALL FAMILY

BIG FAMILY
Mother
Father
Son
Daughter
Grand Mother
Grand Father

SMALL FAMILY

BIG FAMILY
Mother
Father
Son
Daughter
Grand Mother
Grand Father

SMALL FAMILY

BIG FAMILY
Mother
Father
Son
Daughter
Grand Mother
Grand Father

SMALL FAMILY

BIG FAMILY
Mother
Father
Son
Daughter
Grand Mother
Grand Father

SMALL FAMILY

Sab chale gaye, tumhari terah.

Mama used to say,
'Ask yourself the same question eleven times,
and you will get the answer.'

I tried once.